The fearless Samurai X welcomes you to Ninjago world!
Are you ready for an adventure?
Colour in each page and complete the activities.

It's hard not to lose your head in the company of skeletons! In each pair of letters, take the one that appears earlier in the alphabet. That's how you'll find out which bony warrior was pranked by his friends!

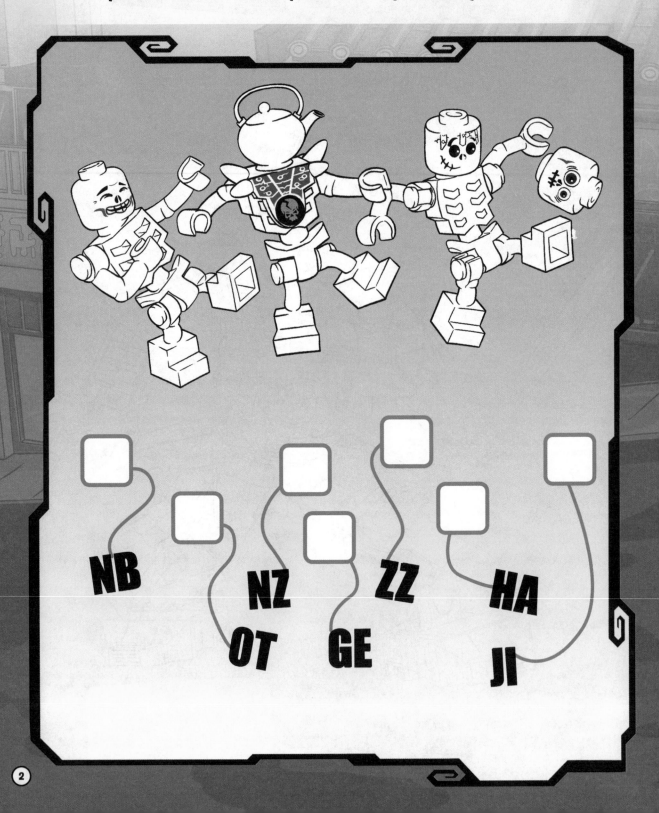

NB

NZ

OT

ZZ

GE

HA

JI

Beware! Nuckal's quad is approaching. Add a sticker of Nya in the empty space and lead her down the path so that no skeleton can catch her!

FINISH

START

**The Ninjago realm is incredibly peaceful –
until the skeletons arrive!**

Use the stickers to show how the Ninjago City residents treat uninvited guests.

No skeleton wants to share his cake with the other skeletons!
Colour in the picture to complete the scene.

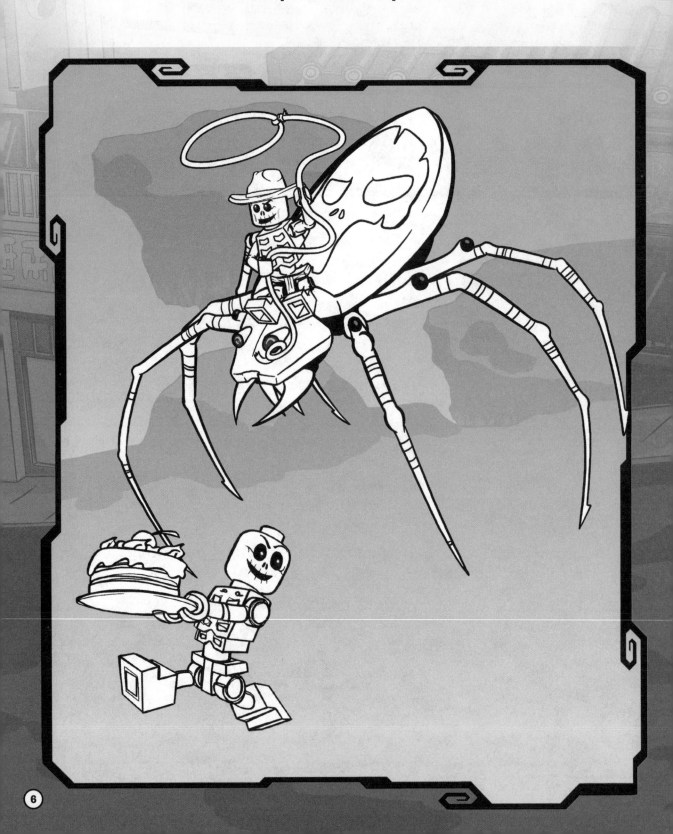

How well do you know all these characters?
Look at each pair and mark the real deal with a tick sticker.

All skeletons want to ride the Skull Motorbike!
Add some skeleton stickers in the queue above it.

If you think defeating the skeletons will give you a moment's rest, you'd better think again! This time, Ninjago City was invaded by the vicious Serpentines! Can you colour the Serpentines green?

The Venomari know that teamwork is important – that's why they came to the Ninjago realm in pairs. Look at the picture and draw lines to connect the identical Serpentines.

The Serpentines have the ninja outnumbered! Luckily for Jay,
not all of them are armed. Count how many snakes have weapons
so that he knows which ones to avoid.

This is how the Serpentines roll in the theme park!
Add letters to match the cut-out fragments to the right places.

A

B

C

Say cheese! Even a Serpentine wants to have a photo with the famous Samurai X!

Look at both scenes and use the arrowhead stickers to mark the five Serpentines who fought in both battles.

There's nothing more zippy than a speedy Rattlecopter. But it won't get far without the right parts! Use the stickers to fill in the missing elements.

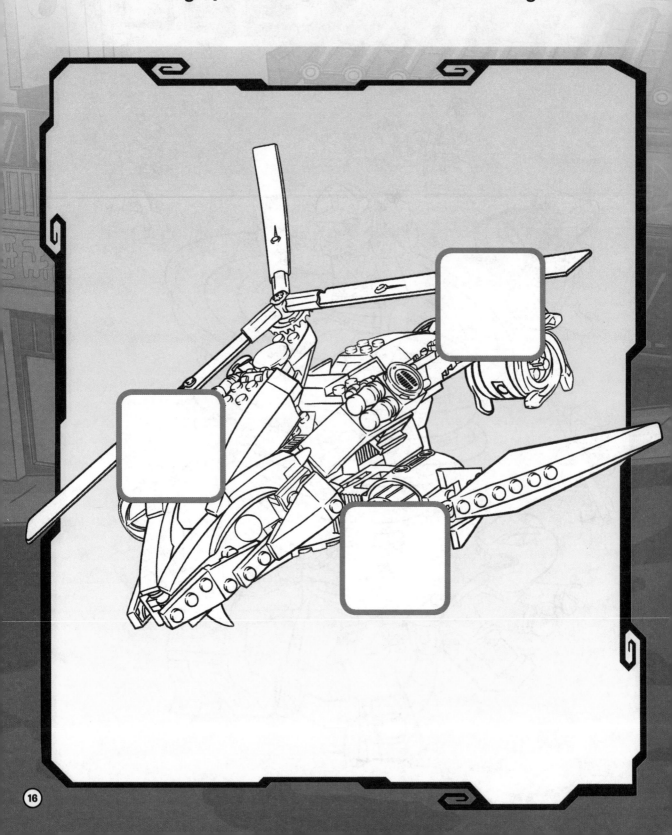

Cyrus Borg shows off his latest invention.
Use the box below to draw in your own Nindroid model.

Washing this huge machine is hard work, even for a robot. It could use your help! Add Nindroid stickers on the page, so there are seven helpers in total!

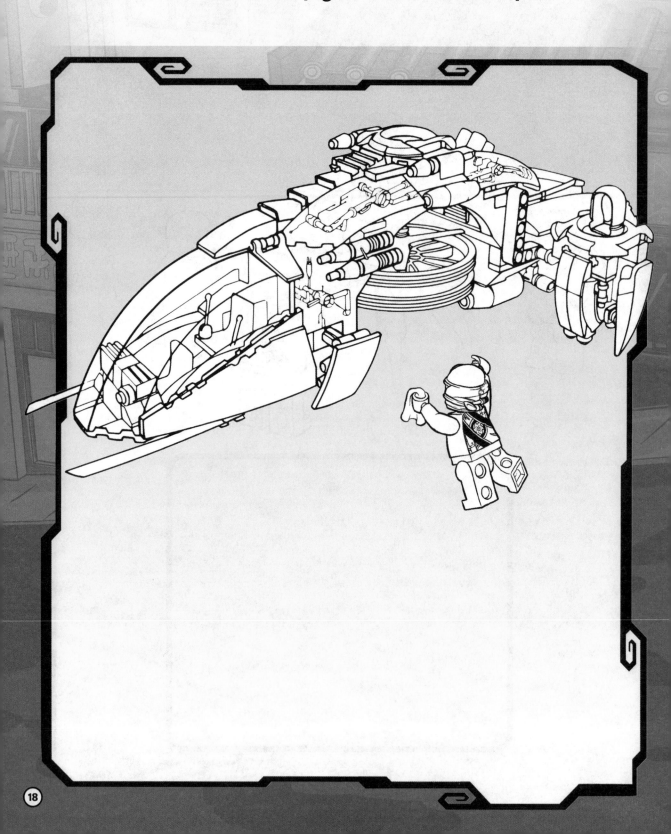

Nindroid production is go! To help build these machines, connect the missing parts with the robots on the assembly line.

Master Wu a villain?
It's the Digital Overlord who turned him into the evil Techno Wu!
Colour the MechDragon purple to complete the scene.

Here comes the Green Ninja!
Add Nindroid stickers to the empty boxes. Then help Lloyd find the correct path to the Nindroid in the Hover Hunter.

A

B

C

D

E

The powerful MechDragon is hovering over Ninjago City. It's accompanied by other minions of the Digital Overlord. It's getting really dangerous!

Find nine differences between the two pictures and mark them with the Nindroid head stickers. Look out for huge, spinning saws!

Who do these Techno Blades belong to? Count the ninja – the one who appears the most times in each column is the owner of the weapon above him.

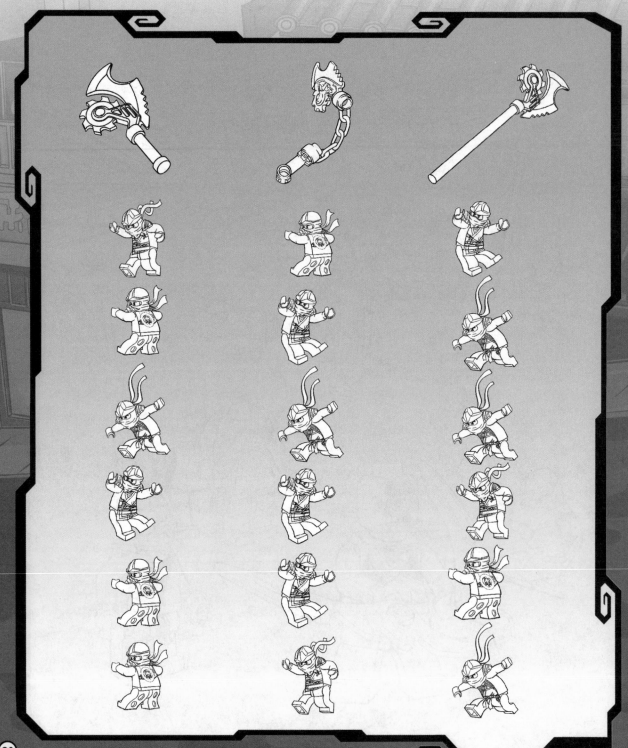

47 47 47 47 47 47

Master Chen, the king of noodles and deception, invites everyone to a grand show. Let the Tournament of Elements begin!

The great arena serves as a fighting ring. The Elemental Masters fight their duels in a grand tournament organised by Chen.

Nothing will stop the upcoming battle! Stick in the Elemental Masters, the ninja and the sneaky cultists. Witness the breath-taking combat!

**The Master of Gravity doesn't juggle his weapons - he just levitates them!
How many more weapons can he deal with?
Give him more sharp equipment from the sticker arsenal!**

Lloyd isn't the only one getting a lift from the helicopter.
Seven monkeys came up with the same idea.
Find them all on Clouse's machine and mark them with monkey stickers!

The Anacondrai Warriors are practising battle formations under the watchful eye of Master Chen. Starting from the second row, circle each new cultist that appears in the rows below.

The cultist has run off with Karlof's huge iron fists.
Help the Master of Metal cross the maze to get them back!

START

FINISH

The sneaky Master Chen was finally defeated!
It's time for a well-deserved rest, so colour in the scene below.

Trouble fell on the City of Stiix – all because of the appearance of Morro
riding a terrifying dragon! Which close-up shows a fragment of the beast?
Mark it with a bat sticker.

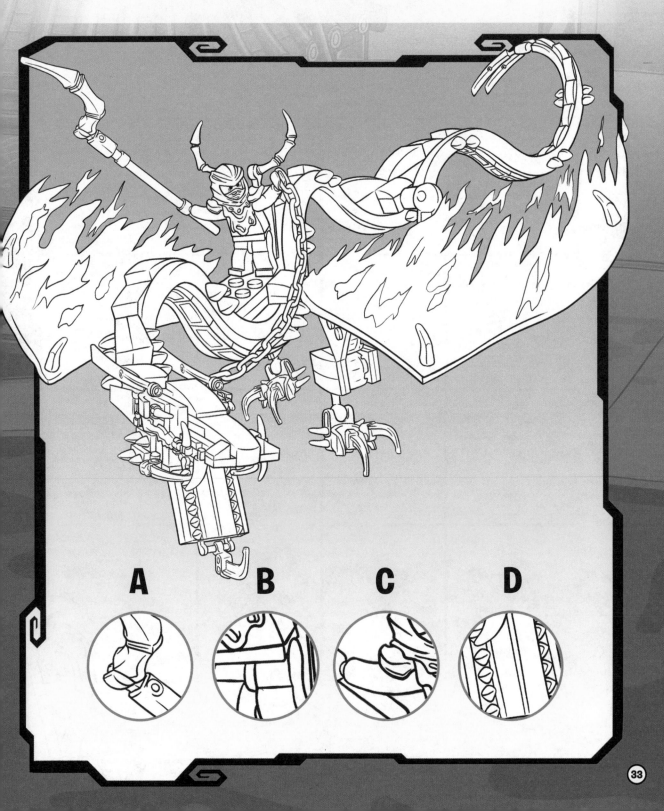

A   B   C   D

Morro did not come alone! Stick in the Ghost Warriors so that none are repeated in any row or column, to discover their secret battle formation!

A true warrior must be strong like a bear, agile like a lizard and perceptive like a hawk! Test your memory - look closely at this picture and then turn the page.

It's time for ninja-style training!
Can you mark the six elements shown on the previous page?
Use the spider stickers and remember - no peeking!

Ghosts don't like *anyone* or *anything*, but if you want to know what this ghost dislikes the most, colour in the shapes marked with an 'x'.

There's an odd ghost out in each group.
Mark it with a ghost warning sticker!

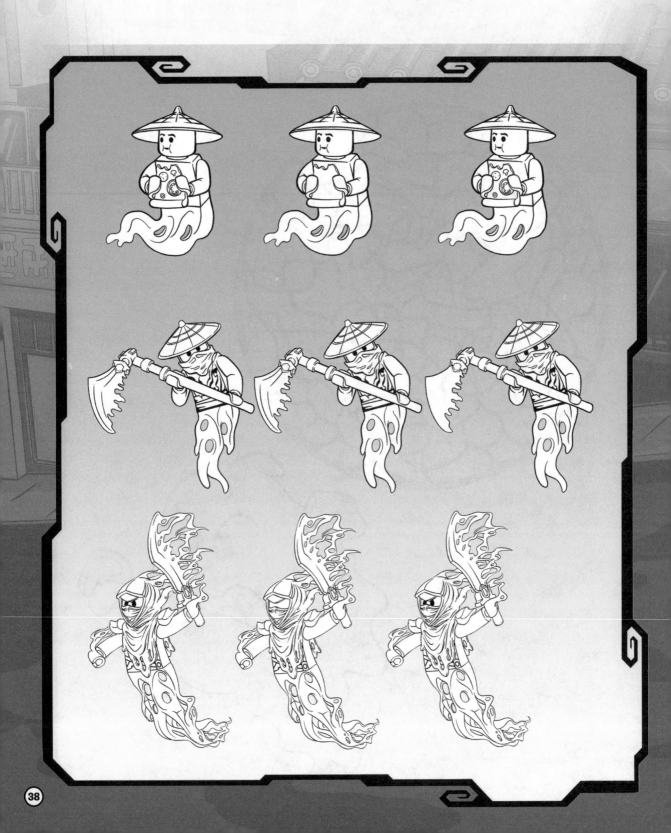

Who tied up this dangerous wraith? Untangle the lines and write the letters in the empty boxes below.

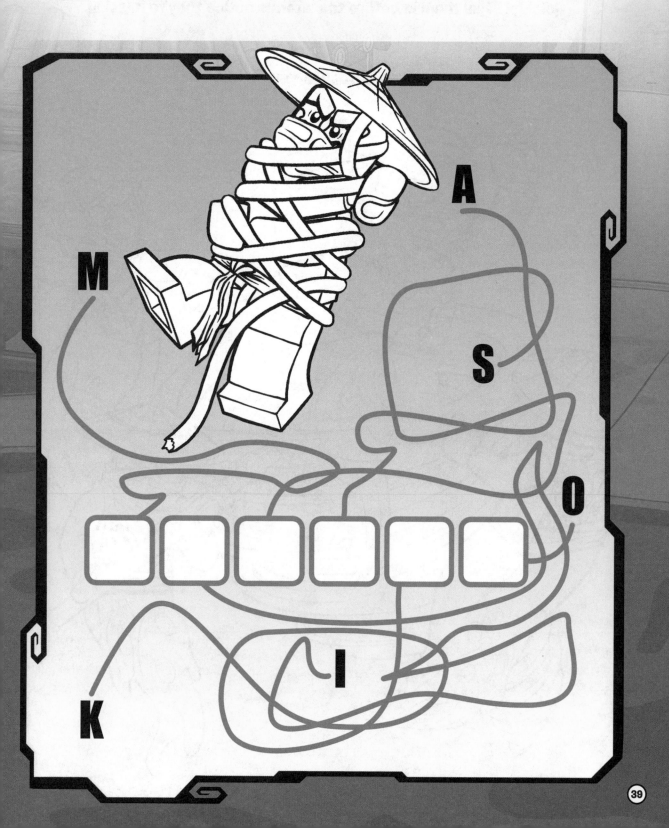

Enemies tremble when Kai enters the scene with his shining,
razor-sharp swords ... Wait a second, where are they?
Quickly! Draw them in before the wraiths notice they're missing.

LEGO, the LEGO logo, the Brick and Knob configurations, the Minifigure and NINJAGO are trademarks of the LEGO Group. ©2016 The LEGO Group. Produced by AMEET Sp. z o.o. under license from the LEGO Group.

Ghosts have hobbies too, when they aren't invading other worlds! Match stickers to the empty spaces so they can have some fun!

Ghosts and ninja are like oil and water - and ghosts just can't stand water!

Take up the ghost challenge! Finish the drawing so that the picture looks just like the small one above it.

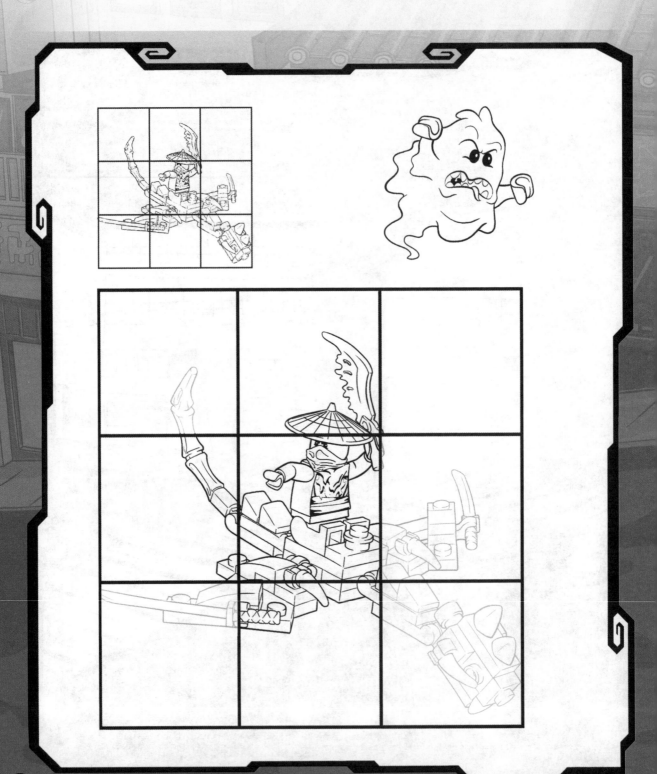

When the situation gets really heated up, there's Ronin to cool it down.
And water, lots of water! Colour in the picture to finish the scene.

Success! After many hardships, the ninja finally have the mysterious scroll. Cole hasn't been in very good spirits, though!

There are 10 differences between the two pictures.
Mark them with stickers of Jay's terrified face.

Nobody can outrun a ghost riding a dragon! Look at the picture fragments at the bottom - can you match them with the right part of the picture?

Nadakhan was imprisoned in a tiny teapot for ages. Follow his trail to find out which teapot it was.

A   B   C

Know your enemy before you face him – every ninja will tell you that. Stick in the pirates next to their descriptions and let the team learn about their new foes.

Stronger than a pirate and a half, she likes the colour blue and carries two pirate flags.

Pilot goggles give him a mysterious look, and a thick black moustache casts fear in sailors' hearts.

One of his numerous misadventures with a mop left him with a wooden leg. His fangs make him mumble a bit.

He's a bit more 'handy' than the rest, likes fancy haircuts and partially covers his face. Your wishes are his command.

Although he vaguely resembles a skeleton, he's much more dangerous. His smile will give you the chills!

Supposedly jail food isn't great, but this was a bit too much for Kai.
Circle seven items that shouldn't have landed on the table!

Add pirate stickers to complete the scene.

**Pirate on the horizon! Jump on the dragon with Jay,
but beware of Cyren's rapid-fire cannon!
Cover all the missiles with lightning stickers so they don't reach the ninja.**

For Clancee, the pirate banner is more important than his favourite mop. That means something! What would your banner look like if you were a pirate captain? Draw it below!

Flintlocke is famous for his eagle eye.
Draw who he's looking at this time!

Nya is a fully-fledged ninja now – she's got her own sword, a new outfit and, most of all, a cool motorcycle to slip past enemies!
Colour in her new motorcycle.

A postman has to do his job, no matter what.
Lead the postman through the maze so he can deliver letters
to the citizens of Ninjago City.

START

FINISH

Dogshank is a real lady – you'd better remember that, or she'll gladly remind you with her favourite anchor. Use the pirate flag sticker to mark the shadow that matches the item in her hands.

This must be the most epic clash in the whole of the Ninjago realm!

Use the stickers to create a legendary battle between the brave ninja and the fearsome pirates.

Jay and Nya make a great team that Ninjago City can always count on!
Sky Pirates, watch out!

Answers

p. 2

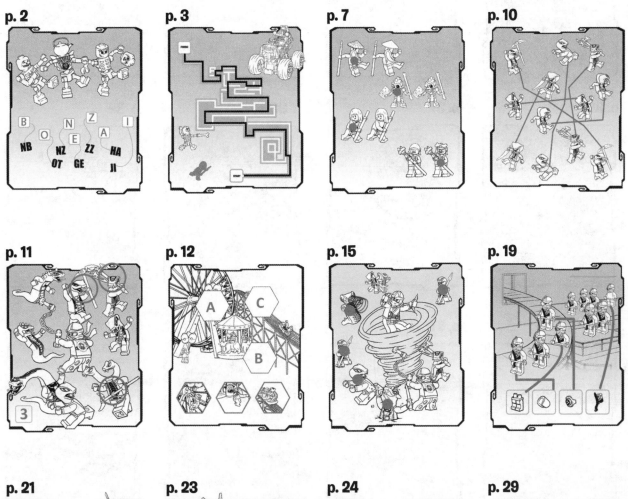

B O N Z A I

NB NZ ZZ HA
OT GE JI

p. 3

p. 7

p. 10

p. 11

3

p. 12

A C

B

p. 15

p. 19

p. 21

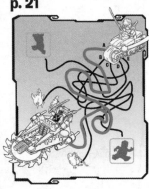

A
B C D E

p. 23

p. 24

p. 29

p. 30

p. 31

p. 33

p. 34

p. 36

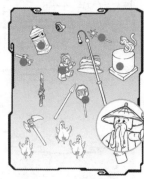

p. 37

p. 38

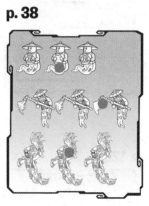

p. 39

p. 41

p. 47

p. 48

p. 49

p. 50

p. 51

p. 58

p. 59